Tacky Goes to Camp

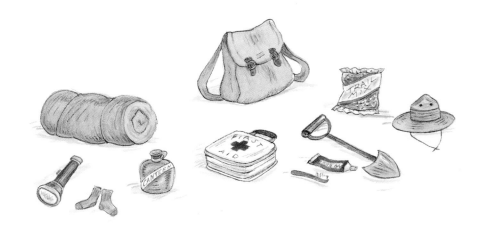

To Betty Gallagher, who after many years in
kindergarten deserves to go to camp!
—H.L.

Text copyright © 2009 by Helen Lester
Illustrations copyright © 2009 by Lynn Munsinger

Houghton Mifflin Books for Children is an imprint of
Houghton Mifflin Harcourt Publishing Company.

www.hmhbooks.com

The text of this book is set in Garamond.

Library of Congress Cataloging-in-Publication Data

Lester, Helen.
Tacky goes to camp / written by Helen Lester and illustrated by Lynn Munsinger.
p. cm.
Summary: Tacky the penguin and his friends go to Camp Whoopihaha where
they scare each other by telling ghost stories around the campfire, never expecting
that one of the frightening stories will come true.
ISBN 978-0-618-98812-9
[1. Camps—Fiction. 2. Bears—Fiction. 3. Penguins—Fiction.] I. Munsinger,
Lynn, ill. II. Title.
PZ7.L56285Taax 2009
[E]—dc22
2008033929

Printed in Singapore
TWP 10 9 8 7 6 5 4 3 2 1

Tacky Goes to Camp

Written by Helen Lester

Illustrated by Lynn Munsinger

Houghton Mifflin Books for Children
Houghton Mifflin Harcourt
Boston 2009

It didn't exactly look like summer camp.

But then, summer didn't exactly look like summer in the Nice Icy Land.

And yet, here were Goodly, Lovely, Angel, Neatly, and Perfect—
and Tacky—
at CAMP WHOOPIHAHA!

Goodly, Lovely, Angel, Neatly and
Perfect had packed carefully.
They brought . . .

Tacky brought . . .

They wore nifty uniforms with their names on them.

And every night they slept in real tents. How campy!

At Whoopihaha their days were filled with wonderful activities.

Rock climbing.

Synchronized swimming.

Archery.

Arts and crafts.

Tacky's personal favorite was a game he invented
called Tippy Canoe and Tacky Too.

But the best activity of all came one evening.
It was Sleep Under the Stars Night.
The penguins gathered around the crackling fire
and sang the camp song*:

We're penguins—we cannot ride horses
Because our legs weren't put on long.
But other than that we're perfection—
Just hear us as we sing our song.
   Whoopi, Whoopi, Whoopihaha ho-ho hee-hee
   Whoopi, Whoopi, Whoopihaha ho-ho.
   (pause)
   Hee-hee.

* To the tune of "My Bonnie Lies Over the Ocean"

Then it was time to make s'mores—toasted marshmallows and chocolate smashed between two graham crackers. Yum.

Finally, just before bedtime, it was SCARY STORY TIME.

Ooooooooo.

Goodly and Lovely told a tale called "Gotcha."

It was about a penguin-poking swordfish, and very scary.

Angel and Neatly came up with "The Creeping, Crawling Plant."
Scarier.

Perfect followed with a story called "The Whooping Wubbawubba Bird," which was so scary the penguins could barely listen, and they held their flippers over their ear-places.

Then it was Tacky's turn.
He announced, "I orey is alled
'Eware uh Air.'"
He unstuck his s'morey beak and
began again.
"My story is called 'Beware the
Bear.'"
That sounded promising.

Tacky began, "Once upon a time the penguins
were gathered around the campfire when they heard a
THUD . . . THUD . . . THUD . . . THUD—
And a Great Growly Voice called out 'Beware the bear.'"

Tacky's companions shivered a little.

"The voice came closer. 'BEWARE THE BEAR.'"
Now the penguins held flippers.

"And closer.
'BEWARE THE BEAR.'"
They squoze their eyes shut and waited.

"And then," said Tacky, "a bear thudded up to the penguins and announced, 'How dee do? My name is Beware. Beware, the bear.' Get it? Yuk yuk. The end."

A silence followed. Then a chorus of "OH."

SCARY STORY TIME had ended as a not-so-scary story night, so the disappointed penguins crawled into their sleeping bags. Only one penguin remained unbagged.

Tacky needed s'more s'mores. At least a few dozen, more or less.
Finally satisfied, he dove in headfirst, not worrying about having
crumbs in his bed.

Nor was he aware that his sleeping bag was lying on the leftovers he
just . . . couldn't . . . quite . . . finnnnish.

Much, much later, well after midnight as the penguins slumbered, there came a THUD . . . THUD . . . THUD . . . THUD . . . and a Great Growly voice boomed out,

"BEWARE THE BEAR."

Up shot Goodly, Lovely, Angel, Neatly, and Perfect, and what they saw was A BEAR. A BEAR TO BEWARE OF.

"Something smells yummy," growled the bear.

He helped himself to one marshmallow, two squares of chocolate, three graham crackers, and four s'more toasting sticks. Then he ate the picnic basket,

gobbled up the guitar,

and swallowed a fire log. Whole.

"NOT YUMMY!" he bellowed. "AND I'M STILL HUNGRY
IN MY TUMMY!"

He hovered over Goodly, Lovely, Angel, Neatly, and Perfect.

The penguins always did everything as a group, and what this group needed to do now was RUN !

But Tacky . . . Tacky . . .

"Wake up! Tacky, wake up!" they cried.
"Want s'more," murmured Tacky from
the depths of his sleeping bag.

"Tacky, wake up!" they repeated.

Frantically they tapped him and poked him.

At last when they tickled his webbies he popped up and . . .

The leftovers upon which Tacky had slept had become stuck to his
sleeping bag, forming a graham-crackery, chocolaty, marshmallowy face.
"Gadzooks!" gasped the bear.
What a horrid-looking thing!
It was huge. With mean eyes. And green skin.
And webbed feet yet.

The bear backed away.
Tacky waddled forward, his muffled voice calling, "Want s'more."
The bear backed farther, falling over a log.
And Tacky continued waddling forward.
"Want s'more."
The terrified bear cried out,
"No more!
I don't want s'more!
No more!"

Yelping, "I'm outta here!" the bear got outta there. Fast.
As he sped off, he thought to himself, *That was embarrassing.*
But at least I'll have a scary story to tell around my campfire
tonight.
Goodly, Lovely, Angel, Neatly, and Perfect hugged Tacky.
They didn't even mind getting sticky.
Tacky was an odd bird, but a nice bird to have around.